≠
Z11b

BENNY AND THE CRAZY CONTEST

BENNY
AND THE
CRAZY CONTEST

BY CHERYL ZACH

Illustrated by Janet Wilson

BRADBURY PRESS
New York

COLLIER MACMILLAN CANADA   Toronto
MAXWELL MACMILLAN INTERNATIONAL PUBLISHING GROUP
New York   Oxford   Singapore   Sydney

Bradbury Press
Macmillan Publishing Company
866 Third Avenue
New York, NY 10022

Collier Macmillan Canada, Inc.
1200 Eglinton Avenue East
Suite 200
Don Mills, Ontario M3C 3N1

Printed and bound in the United States of America
First Edition
10 9 8 7 6 5 4 3 2 1

The text of this book is set in 14 point Caledonia.
The illustrations are rendered in pencil.
Book design by Sarah Vure and Cathy Bobak

LIBRARY OF CONGRESS CATALOGING-IN-PUBLICATION DATA
Zach, Cheryl.
Benny and the crazy contest / by Cheryl Zach.
p.   cm.
Summary: Ten-year-old Benny Holt enters a contest to win a new bicycle.
ISBN 0-02-793705-4
[1. Contests—Fiction.   2. Bicycles and bicycling—Fiction.
3. Family life—Fiction.]   I. Title.
PZ7.Z165Be   1991
[Fic]—dc20   90-43903

*For two important men in my
life, to whom Benny owes
more than a little: my son,
Quinn Wasden, and my
brother, Richard Byrd, with
love and admiration*

CONTENTS

NO GOOD

Benny Holt sat on his front step and stared at his bike. Look at all those scratches on the fender, from the time he'd run into the mailbox. The front tire was flat. Worse than that, when he got on, Benny's feet hung all the way down to the ground. This bike was too small for someone who was almost ten years old.

1

Next door, Melissa Wong had a new bike, even though she only came to Benny's eyebrows. It was red and shiny and had all-terrain tires. She'd gotten it for her tenth birthday at the beginning of summer. Now she rode down the edge of Tulip Street, zipping around the palm trees, and waved as she went by.

"Come ride with me," she called.

"Can't," Benny said.

"Why not?"

Benny pretended not to hear.

Murray down the street was eleven. He had a new bike, too, a mountain bike. It was blue and gleamed even brighter than Melissa's.

Murray zoomed by next, almost running into Melissa.

"Hey, watch it!" she yelled as her bike wobbled.

"Bet I can outrace you," Murray shouted to Benny.

Benny pretended not to hear. He hadn't

ridden his bike all week, but today still wasn't a good day for riding a too-small bike. He pushed his bike back to the garage. Inside the door, he saw an old catalog on top of a stack of newspapers waiting to be recycled. Benny flipped through the pages. Maybe he could save his allowance and buy a new bike. He got a dollar a week.

But when he found the bikes, Benny shook his head. There was a big number next to the bike he wanted. That would take lots and lots of weeks.

Benny put the catalog back. Outside, he saw his mom in the back garden, tying up her tomato plants. She handled the big, bushy plants with their small, green tomatoes very carefully.

"Mom," Benny said, hurrying over. "I need a new bike. My old bike's all scratched up. It has a flat tire."

"Put some air in the tire," Mom said. "I'll buy you some paint for the scratches."

Benny frowned. His mother tied another tall tomato plant to a wooden stake.

"It's too small," Benny told her. "What about for my birthday?"

"Oh, Benny." Mom sighed and pushed her glasses back up her nose. "I'm sorry. Not this year. You know there's no money for a new bike. Your dad was laid off for three months in the spring, remember? Now go weed the flower bed."

Benny's dad worked in a factory making parts for airplanes. Sometimes he did such a good job that there were too many parts, and he would be laid off.

Benny kicked a clod of dirt. He stamped over to the back door and sat down on the step. Then the door banged, and his fourteen-year-old sister, Angie, came out. Benny jumped out of the way. She had one side of her red hair wrapped around electric curlers. The other side hung down around her neck. She had baby Kevin and a large tote bag under one arm, and she dragged his walker out the door with the other.

Kevin reached for his big brother. Benny ducked. "You're supposed to be watching Kevin, not me," he told Angie.

"He's trashing my room," she explained. "I can't even do my hair. You take him, just for five minutes."

"No way," Benny told her. "It's your turn. Unless—"

"Unless what?"

"You'd like to lend me some money," Benny suggested.

"How much?"

"Enough for a new bike?"

"Are you kidding?" Angie shook her head, and one curler slipped out of place. She pushed it back. "If I had that much money, I'd buy a new denim jacket."

Angie put Kevin back into his walker and pointed him toward the grass. Kevin pushed the walker slowly up and down the lawn.

Angie plopped down beside Benny and pulled a can of mousse out of her bag. She sprayed the gunky stuff into her hair.

"I hate my hair," Angie told him. "Red, and no curls at all."

Benny touched his own short hair. "What's wrong with red hair?"

"And my freckles. I tried lemon juice to fade them, but it didn't work."

Benny crossed his eyes, trying to see the end of his nose. "What's wrong with freckles?"

Angie ignored him. She pulled a magazine out of her tote bag and turned to a page full of hairstyles.

On the opposite page, Benny saw the words *BIG PRIZES*. He opened his eyes wide. "Hey!"

JUST RIGHT

"What's wrong with you?" Angie demanded.

Benny was too excited to answer. In the middle of the page, he saw a picture of a bike—and what a beauty! He stared at the glossy picture, ignoring the car and the furniture and the cameras around it. The bike had everything a mountain bike should have, and it was blue, just right for Benny.

Benny picked up the magazine. "Can I borrow this?"

Angie frowned. "*May* I borrow this," she corrected, sounding just like their mother. "Why?"

"It's important," he told her. "I want to enter the contest. Please?"

"If you'll watch Kevin for five minutes while I change clothes," Angie told him. "I'm going over to Susan's after dinner."

"Hurry up," Benny said. He knew that Angie trying on clothes took even longer than Angie fixing her hair.

"You'd better hurry," Angie said. "I read about that contest. The deadline is to-morrow."

Tomorrow! Oh, wow. He studied the magazine after Angie went inside.

"Win fantastic prizes," it said in big letters. "Enter our easy contest. Write, 'Why I like Potter's Peanut Butter' in forty-five words or less." Benny didn't bother reading the fine print at the bottom of the page.

He didn't have much time. Still, this contest didn't sound very hard. Benny ate Potter's Peanut Butter all the time. He thought about an entry. "I like peanut butter because—"

Kevin fussed. Benny looked up at the baby. Kevin's walker had hit a ridge of grass. He was stuck.

"Push harder," Benny told him. He thought about peanut butter some more. "I like peanut butter because it tastes great."

He shook his head. Not good enough.

"Because it's thick and chewy and sticks to the top of your mouth."

The judges might not like that. Contests were harder than he thought.

He heard a plop, then Kevin wailed. Not again! Benny looked up. Kevin had pushed so hard that he'd turned the walker over, falling face first onto the grass. Benny jumped up and hurried to pick up the baby.

He brushed a piece of grass off Kevin's freckled nose.

"You're okay," Benny told his brother.

Kevin hiccuped. "Mama," he said, holding out his arms toward his mother.

"Good idea," Benny muttered. How would he ever finish his contest entry on time with all these interruptions?

Mrs. Holt wiped her hands on her jeans and picked up the baby, kissing his sore nose. "All better," she murmured.

Benny went back to his contest, but he couldn't think of anything to say. He'd never win a bike like this.

He heard footsteps on the driveway. Grandpa was home. Grandpa's hair was gray, not red, but he was a Holt, too.

"Hi," Benny said. "What's up?"

"Bingo at the Senior Citizens' Center." Grandpa beamed. "Look what I won." He held up a small white lamp.

"Not bad," Benny said politely.

Grandpa showed the lamp to Mrs. Holt.

"How pretty," she said. "Are you going to put it in your bedroom?"

Grandpa had his own room, built onto the back of the garage.

On his mother's hip Kevin reached for the lamp. Grandpa pulled it back.

"I thought you could use it in the living room," Grandpa suggested generously.

"Thank you," Mrs. Holt said. "That room needs all the help it can get."

Mrs. Holt took the baby and the new lamp inside. Benny showed the magazine to his grandfather.

"I want to win a new bike," Benny explained. "I have to write 'Why I like Potter's Peanut Butter' in forty-five words or less. But I can't think of a good reason."

Grandpa shook his head. "Can't help you there," he said. "Can't eat peanut butter, myself. It gets under my false teeth. I like peanut butter cookies, though. In fact, they sound mighty tasty." Grandpa headed for the kitchen.

Benny clicked his teeth together, glad *he* still had all his teeth. He told himself he'd brush extra hard before going to bed. He went to get a pencil and piece of paper, then sat back down with the magazine and tried to think.

It wasn't long before his mother called, "Dinner."

Another interruption!

In the kitchen, Benny's dad sat at the head of the table. He still wore his blue work clothes.

"Hi, Dad," Benny said. "My bike has a flat tire."

"Put some air in it," his dad told him. "You know where the tire pump is."

They ate meat loaf and noodles and peas and salad. Benny ate his meat loaf and noodles and peas, then pushed the salad around his plate.

Kevin sat in his high chair, throwing peas across the room. One landed in the middle of Benny's salad.

"Eat your salad, Benny," his mother said.

"I can't," Benny told her. "Kevin threw his yucky pea into it."

Shaking her head, Mrs. Holt brought out dessert. "Grandpa made peanut butter cookies," she told them.

"Good!" Benny said.

Angie nodded, and Kevin clapped his hands. "Cookie!"

Everyone ate bowls of vanilla ice cream with peanut butter cookies, still warm from the oven.

"Good job, Dad," Mr. Holt said.

Benny liked the cookies, too. But he needed ideas for his contest entry.

"Tell me something good about peanut butter," he asked his mother.

"It's a good source of protein," she said. She picked a pea out of Kevin's nose. "I use it in my special recipe for meat loaf."

Peanut butter meat loaf, hmm. Benny looked around the table. "What else?"

"One of my magazines had a peanut butter and oatmeal facial," Angie said. "It faded Susan's freckles. Didn't work on mine, though." She wrinkled her nose in disgust.

Benny was thinking about peanut butter, not freckles. "I didn't know you could use peanut butter for so many different things—cookies, meat loaf, freckle facials." He pulled his pencil and paper out of his pocket and wrote it all down.

Angie stood up and took a jar of peanut butter from the pantry, setting it on the table. "I like it on crackers," she said. "But only a few. It'll make you fat."

"Try it with pickles," Grandpa suggested.

Benny made a face. Ugg. He didn't like pickles.

Dad cleared his throat. "Try a spoonful in your hot chocolate," Dad told him.

16

Benny wrote it down.

Angie giggled. "Look at Kevin," she said.

Mrs. Holt clucked her tongue and reached for the baby. Kevin had his fingers into the peanut butter. Now he rubbed the brown goo over his high chair.

"Finger painting with peanut butter, that's something for your list, Benny," Grandpa said, chuckling.

"What a mess," Mrs. Holt said. She lifted Kevin out of the high chair and took him away for his bath.

"Thanks for all the ideas," Benny told his family. "You've helped a lot."

"Angie," Mrs. Holt called from the bathroom. "You can wash the dishes."

"I have to go over to Susan's," Angie protested. "We're going to watch videos on TV."

"Dishes first," their mother said.

Benny grinned.

"Benny can dry," their mother added.

Benny stopped grinning.

"Ha," Angie told him. "I'll stack the dishes. You sweep the peas off the floor."

Benny went to get the broom. All those good contest ideas—but none of them were his. What should he do?

FORTY-FIVE WORDS OR LESS

Angie washed and Benny dried. Then Angie left for Susan's house. Alone in the kitchen, Benny dried the last pot. He could hear Grandpa in the living room talking to his mom. Where was Dad?

As if in answer, he heard Dad call, "Benny! Can you come here for a minute?"

Benny headed for the garage. His dad was

busy at his workbench, taking apart the old brown lamp from the living room.

"Want to help me?"

"Sure," Benny said, coming closer. "What's wrong with it?"

"Needs new wires," Dad explained. He put down the lamp and reached for the box of toothpicks he kept on the top shelf. He took out one and put it in his mouth. He offered the box to Benny.

Benny took a toothpick and chewed on it, letting it dangle from the side of his mouth, just like his dad.

Mr. Holt reached inside his toolbox for a pair of pliers. Benny watched as his dad took apart the base of the lamp and removed the damaged wiring. His dad's hands were strong and wide, but they handled the wiring and the tools skillfully, never making a mistake.

Benny got to help hold the wire in place. When they finished, Dad put the base back onto the lamp and plugged it into the electric outlet. The lamp blinked on right away.

"We did it," Benny said, dropping his toothpick. He grinned.

Dad nodded.

"I could do that," Benny added.

"No, no," his dad told him. "You *never* touch electric wiring unless I'm with you. Electricity is dangerous."

When his dad spoke in that tone, Benny always listened.

"Sure," he agreed.

"Finished your peanut butter contest yet?" Dad asked him.

"Not yet," Benny said. "And I'm running out of time. What's the weirdest way you ever used peanut butter?"

Mr. Holt thought about it. "Once, when I was fishing and I ran out of bait, I stuck some peanut butter and bread from my lunch onto a hook."

Benny laughed. Peanut butter for fish! "Did you catch anything?"

"Well, no," his dad admitted.

"I guess fish don't care for peanut butter," Benny decided.

"Maybe not."

Mr. Holt straightened his workbench, and they headed inside. "Promised Dad I'd play a game of checkers," he told Benny. "Want to play the winner?"

"Sure." Benny knew the checker game would last awhile. Both his dad and grandpa were champion checker players. He'd work on his contest entry while he waited.

He didn't have much time, and he just had to win that bike!

Friday morning Benny tried again to finish his contest entry. "I like Potter's Peanut Butter because it makes a special meat loaf." That was his mom's idea.

"I like Potter's Peanut Butter because you

can use it in a facial to fade your freckles," he wrote. That was Angie's idea. Which one was best?

Benny stared at his paper, then tried again. "I like Potter's Peanut Butter because it makes good cookies (Grandpa), you can use it for cocoa or for finger painting (Dad and baby Kevin)." Which one to pick?

From having no ideas, now he had too many. Benny put his paper back into his pocket and shook his head.

His mother came to the bedroom door. "Take Kevin for his walk, please."

"I took him yesterday."

"No, you didn't," Angie called from her room. "I did!"

Benny groaned. The only bad part about summer vacation was that he had to help with the baby. He put Kevin into his stroller. Kevin's short legs went the wrong way— both sticking out one side. "Wa-wa!" Kevin cried.

"Hold on," Benny said. As he bent over, the paper in his jeans pocket fell out. The baby grabbed it and tried to take a bite.

"Hey," Benny scolded. "You can't eat my contest entry." He took the paper from Kevin and thrust it deeper into his pocket. He picked up the baby and seated him the right way, then pushed the stroller out to the sidewalk.

"Hi, Benny," Melissa called. She rode her new red bike past them. Her long black hair blew in the wind.

Every time he came outside, Melissa and Murray showed up on their bikes. Benny wondered darkly if they did it on purpose. What did they do—circle the block, waiting for him to come out, just to remind him that he didn't have a new bike, too? He bent over the stroller and refused to answer.

"Good morning, young man." Mrs. Wong looked up from her rose garden.

"Hey," Murray shouted. He rode by on

his new mountain bike. "Look how fast I can go!"

Benny gritted his teeth.

"Want to race?" Murray asked.

"I'm busy."

"Benny the baby-sitter." Murray laughed.

Benny put his head down and pushed faster. The stroller hit a crack in the sidewalk, and Kevin bounced too hard. "Wa-wa-wa," he complained.

"All right," Benny told him. They slowed down. Mrs. Morales's little dog ran to greet them. Kevin stopped yelling and grabbed for the dog's ears. The dog backed away. Smart dog.

"We're almost home again," Benny told the baby. They had circled the block. When they reached their own driveway, Kevin started again, "Wa-wa-wa."

"Say Ma-ma," Benny suggested.

Kevin didn't listen. "Wa-wa-wa."

"No more," Benny told him. "I've got to

finish my contest entry. Anyhow, it's time for your nap, I hope."

Mrs. Holt took the baby. Benny sat down and thought over all his family's suggestions. He still didn't know which one to pick for the contest. Time was running out.

Wham! Banging came from the garage. Dad was at work, and Mom was in the bedroom with Kevin. What was Grandpa doing? Benny went to see. He wasn't in his bedroom behind the garage. At the workbench at the other end, Grandpa hammered a big sheet of cardboard to a long piece of wood. It said, "Vote for Bob Hawkins."

"What's that?" Benny wanted to know.

"Bob Hawkins talked to the senior citizens last week," Grandpa told him. "Clever man. Wants to expand the Senior Citizens' Center, spend more money on the parks. He's running for city council. I'm going to help him. If people stick together, no telling what we can do."

Benny looked at the signs Grandpa had made. One said, "Hawkins is the man for the job." Another said, "Hawkins works hard."

"Good signs," Benny said. He thought about Grandpa's slogans. Maybe this was what he needed. He went outside, away from the noise, took out his paper, and started again.

"I like Potter's Peanut Butter because it's the best butter for the job," he wrote. "My family uses it lots of ways."

Benny shook his head. Not quite. "Potter's works hard," he wrote. That didn't make sense. Benny chewed on the end of his pencil and thought about giving up. Then he remembered the beautiful bike in the magazine. No way!

There was a dark smear on his piece of paper—Kevin's sticky fingers again. Benny remembered Kevin and the peanut butter. He grinned and jumped to his feet.

That was it!

LOSING

Benny wrote in big letters, "Potter's Peanut Butter makes my whole family stick together."

Would they know what he meant? Benny wrinkled his nose in thought, then started over. "Potter's Peanut Butter is the best. We all like it: peanut butter meat loaf (Mom), peanut butter face goo (Angie), peanut butter cookies (Grandpa), peanut butter cocoa (Dad), peanut butter finger paint (Kevin), and peanut butter sandwiches (me). Potter's helps my family stick together."

He counted carefully. Forty-four words! And he'd worked it out all by himself. Well, almost.

Benny whooped with excitement and hurried into the hall to show his sister. "Read it," Benny told her. "I finally finished."

Angie took the phone from her ear long enough to glance over his sheet of paper. "Not bad," she told him.

Not bad? What kind of crack was that? But as Benny hurried to get the magazine from Angie's room, he heard her say into the phone, "Guess what, Susan. My brother actually thought of something pretty smart."

That was better. Benny borrowed Angie's pen and copied his forty-four words neatly onto the official entry blank. At the bottom, he added, "I want the bike, please."

Angie finally hung up the phone and came to look over his shoulder.

"An adult has to sign the entry form," she told him.

"How come?" Benny shouted.

"Sshh," Angie reminded him. "You'll wake the baby."

"But I have to mail it today," Benny repeated, not so loud. "Where's Mom?"

"She walked up to the grocery store. She'll be back soon. The mail on the corner doesn't go until four o'clock."

Benny cut the entry blank carefully out of the magazine, then soaked a peanut butter jar in hot water until he could peel off the label. Angie found an envelope and stamp. She wrote the address on the envelope and Benny licked the stamp.

His mom still wasn't home. Benny looked at the big clock on the kitchen wall. Twenty minutes till four o'clock. Hurry, Mom!

He went outside and paced up and down

the driveway, watching impatiently for his mother. When he saw Mrs. Holt coming, her arms full of grocery bags, Benny ran to help her. He grabbed one of the bags. "Hurry," he panted.

"Is something wrong with the baby?" Mrs. Holt sounded anxious.

"No." Benny lugged the heavy bag inside to the kitchen table, then handed her his entry. "Sign this," he said.

"What is it?" His mother put down her bag.

"It's for my contest entry," Benny explained. His mother took a pen and signed her name on the line. Benny licked the envelope shut, then ran all the way to the corner and dropped the envelope into the big blue mailbox. Just in time. A white mail van pulled up even as he let the entry slip inside.

Whew! Benny watched the postal worker load the mail into big green duffle bags, making sure the man didn't accidentally drop his contest entry, then walked slowly home.

"How long till I find out if I won?" he asked his sister.

Angie studied the magazine. "The end of July," she told him.

Benny groaned. "That's over a month!"

Angie shook her head. "You still won't win, you know. Lots of people have good entries."

"Not as good as mine," Benny told her.

But a whole month!

July was the longest month Benny had ever spent. Dad worked lots of overtime. Mom tended the garden and cooked fresh green beans and squash. The tomatoes grew rounder and plumper and began to turn color. Kevin took his first step. Melissa went away to visit her grandmother. Murray was his usual self. Benny didn't have anything to do.

He finally decided to ride his old, too-small bike. Benny found the tire pump and pumped air into the front tire. When he got on, he had to crunch his legs up to fit on the pedals. Benny shook his head. "This bike gets smaller every day."

Murray rode by on his mountain bike. *His* legs didn't hang all the way to the ground.

"Ready to race?" he called.

"Don't want to," Benny said. He pushed the pedals hard, trying to leave Murray behind.

But Murray skimmed ahead. "You're just afraid I'll beat you," he said.

"Am not," Benny told him.

"Are too."

"All right." Benny gave in. "At the park?"

"Sure," Murray said. He zipped ahead on his big bike.

Benny made a face. The wheels on Murray's bike were so big, and Benny's wheels were so small.

The park was two blocks away. They rode

past the swing sets and the sandbox. Past the slide and the monkey bars.

Past the ballpark.

Next came the sand hills—just right for climbing and sliding down. Just right for a mountain bike. Too high for a little bike like Benny's.

"Wow!" Murray yelled. "Here comes Murray, the dive-bomber!"

He rode his bike very fast up the first hill. So fast, his wheels blurred.

Benny pushed hard on the pedals. He almost didn't make it up the hill.

Murray bounced over the top, his bike almost flying. "This is great," he called.

Benny didn't think so. His tires slid in the soft sand, and his legs ached.

Murray coasted quickly down the hill. His big bike wobbled as he started up the next slope.

Benny was falling behind. He tried to pedal faster.

Murray went up the second hill and over the top. He went down even faster, then hit a rock.

The big bike bounced sideways.

"Yow!" Murray yelled. He tumbled off his bike, and the bike fell on top of him.

Benny couldn't stop.

"Look out!" He slid into Murray's bike.

"Ouch!" Murray shouted.

Benny shot forward over the top of his bike and slid in the sand. He didn't have any breath to yell with. His knee hit the frame of the bike. Did it hurt!

When he sat up, he rubbed sand out of his face and checked his knee. A long scratch dripped blood through a ragged tear in his jeans. He looked at his bike. The front tire was flat again.

He looked at Murray's bike. The bright blue paint had a big scratch. Benny almost felt sorry for Murray.

Murray frowned. "This is all your fault,"

he said hotly. "You ran right into me."

"You hit the rock first," Benny told him. "I didn't make you fall." He didn't feel so sorry anymore.

Murray rubbed his arm. He picked up his bike and scowled at the scratch on the front. "Anyhow, I beat you," he said. He rode away.

"Did not," Benny yelled. "Doesn't count. You fell off!"

His knee hurt. Drops of blood dripped onto the dirt. He picked up his bike and began to push it home, limping.

"You wait," Murray shouted. "I'll beat you again, every single day!"

It took Benny a long time to walk home. He pushed his bike into the garage and went looking for his mother. She would say, "What did you do to your knee?" Then she would tell him to wash it off and put on a Band-Aid.

His mother wasn't in the kitchen. She

wasn't in the living room. Angie was in the hall talking on the telephone.

"Where's Mom?" Benny asked.

"Next door, having coffee with Mrs. Wong."

Kevin was asleep in his crib. Benny went into the bedroom, careful not to make noise. He took off his torn jeans, went to the bathroom, and washed off his scraped knee. The soapy water stung. He put a Band-Aid over the scratch. No more bike riding, Benny decided.

When July finally ended, Benny sat on the doorstep every day and waited for the mail carrier. When she arrived, Benny checked the mail, but no letters came from the contest.

Benny decided the contest had forgotten about his entry. Maybe it had been lost. He was never going to win his new bike.

Then one day, Benny was in the living

room, playing roll the ball with Kevin. The phone rang.

Benny heard his mother answer.

"Yes, this is Elizabeth Holt. What? I didn't enter any contest. You've got the wrong number."

"No, Mom!" Benny ran for the hall.

WINNING

Too late. Benny's mother hung up.

Benny felt sick.

His mother stared at him. "Why are you shouting?"

"That was my entry for the peanut butter contest," Benny told her. "Remember when you signed it? Now they'll never bring my bike."

"Oh, Benny," his mother said. "I forgot all about that. I'm really sorry."

Benny wondered who would get his new bike now. Whoever it was, that kid couldn't want a new bike as bad as he did.

The phone rang again. They both grabbed for it, but his mom got there first. Benny jumped up and down.

"Yes, this is Elizabeth Holt. I'm sorry, I'd forgotten about the entry. Yes, we'll be home tomorrow."

When she hung up, she smiled at Benny. "They'll deliver the prize Thursday."

"I won, I won!" Benny jumped up and down. His mother laughed and took his hands, and they danced around the table together.

Tomorrow he'd get his bike!

Benny woke up before the sun on Thursday morning. He pulled on his clothes in the dark bedroom and ran for the front door.

His mother found him sitting on the doorstep. She pulled her robe tighter and gave him a hug. "Come eat some breakfast."

Benny went to the table and gulped down two spoonfuls of cereal. "I have to watch for the truck."

He went back to the front step. Tulip Street looked deserted, and the early morning sunlight shone bright and clear. Benny waited patiently.

In a while, Melissa rode over on her red bike. "Want to play?"

Benny shook his head. "I'm waiting for my new bike," he told her. "I won it in the peanut butter contest."

Melissa looked impressed. She sat down to wait with him.

Angie came to the door, yawning. "I still can't believe you really won."

Benny grinned.

She sat down on the step, too. The three of them waited for the truck.

They sat there a long time. The sun rose higher and brighter and hotter.

"I'm going home," Melissa said. "You probably made it all up."

Benny stuck out his tongue at her back.

Benny and Angie waited. Two trucks went by, but they didn't stop at Benny's house.

Angie stood up. "I think you dreamed that phone call," she said. "I'm going to curl my hair."

Benny waited all by himself.

Benny's mother came to the door. "Don't you want some lunch? A peanut butter sandwich?"

Benny's stomach rumbled at the thought of food, but he shook his head.

Then a big truck drove down Tulip Street, followed by a red car. The truck slowed, then turned into Benny's driveway. The car pulled in behind it. A young lady got out, carrying a big camera.

Benny's heart beat fast.

"Is this Mrs. Elizabeth Holt's house?" the young woman asked.

Benny nodded.

She waved to the two men in the truck. "Bring out the prize."

"Mom!" Benny found his voice. "They're here."

Benny's mother hurried to the door, with Angie behind her. They both stared at the truck.

"My goodness," Benny's mother said.

Angie's eyes were big.

"A dream, huh?" Benny said.

"Mrs. Elizabeth Holt?" the young woman asked. "I have your wonderful prize from the Potter's Peanut Butter contest. Sign here, please."

"It was Benny who really won," Mrs. Holt explained. She signed a bunch of papers.

Melissa ran across the yard.

"It did come!" she said, surprised. "You really did win."

"Told you," Benny said proudly.

They all watched as the truck driver and his partner opened the big doors in the back of the truck. The two men climbed inside.

Benny held his breath.

The men came back into view. They carried out a white and pink flowered couch.

NO EXCHANGES ALLOWED

A couch?

"Oh, how pretty," Mrs. Holt said. "Furniture, too?"

"Where would you like us to put this, ma'am?" the driver asked.

Benny's mother showed them into the living room. The two men put down the new couch. They took the old couch with the hole in the cushion and carried it out to the garage.

Then they went back to the truck.

Benny waited for his new bike.

The driver brought out a pink chair.

"Terrific," Angie said.

The man took the new chair inside the house. He moved the old brown chair out to the garage.

Benny waited for his bike.

The two men brought out a long, rolled-up rug. A pair of lamps. Tables.

Benny's mother and sister oohed and aahed over the new furniture. The young woman pulled out a notebook and asked lots of silly questions, like, "How does it feel to be a winner?"

"Ask Benny," Mrs. Holt said.

Benny frowned at the young lady, but she took his picture, anyhow. She took pictures of Mrs. Holt and Angie and Kevin sitting on the new couch.

"Benny," his mother called. "Don't you want to be in the picture with us?"

Benny shook his head. He was still waiting for his bike.

Then the truck driver shut the big doors of the truck.

"Where's my bike?" Benny demanded.

The man looked at him, surprised. "Bike?"

"The bike I won in the contest."

The man shook his head. "You didn't win the bike, son," he said. "Your mother won the new living room set. Much nicer prize."

"Wait," Mrs. Holt said. "Can't we exchange the furniture for a bike for Benny?"

"Mother!" Angie protested.

The young lady shook her head. "Sorry. Contest rules won't allow it."

The two men drove away. The young lady took one last picture, then she drove off, too.

Benny thought he might cry. He was too old to cry, but he had a big lump in his throat.

"Oh, Benny, I'm really sorry." His mother hugged him.

"You've got the furniture," Angie pointed out.

Benny sniffed. "You can have the furniture," he told his mother. "I don't want it."

"Thank you, Benny. I love the new living room set. Thank you for winning it."

Benny felt a little better. But what about his new bike?

When Grandpa got home, he was surprised to see the new living room furniture. So was Dad.

"That must have been a super good entry." Dad patted Benny on the back.

Grandpa grinned. "Sure beats my little lamp as a prize."

Benny's mother was very proud of the new rug and the new furniture.

When Benny came in from digging weeds out of the flowers, she said, "Don't walk on the new rug in your dirty shoes!"

Benny took off his shoes, then sat down on the new white and pink couch.

"Don't sit on the new couch in your dirty jeans," Mom called.

Benny went out to the garage and sat on the old couch with the hole in the cushion. He stared at the block wall and thought about contests. Contests were rotten.

In a few minutes Angie came out, too.

"Mom won't let me paint my nails in the living room," she complained. "She won't even let me read my magazines. She says they'll turn the couch black."

She moved a lampshade and sat down on the other side of the old couch.

Grandpa soon followed. "Your mother's new furniture has gone to her head," he said. "She won't let me put my feet on the table."

"I wanted to see *Gone with the Wind* on TV tonight," Angie grumbled.

Grandpa got his black and white TV from his bedroom. He put the TV on a box, then moved a couple of boxes off the old brown chair and sat down.

Angie didn't like *Gone with the Wind* in black and white. "I can't see the colors of the dresses."

"Stop grumbling," Grandpa said.

Dad came next. "Your mother won't let me eat my cookies in the living room, said I dropped crumbs on the rug."

He sat on a box. They all crowded into the end of the garage.

In a little while Benny's mother came out of the house. They all looked at her.

"I miss you." She sighed. "My new furniture is very nice, but I like my family better. Angie, you can read your magazines in the living room, but you can't paint your nails."

"All right." Angie nodded.

"Grandpa, you can put your feet up if you'll take off your shoes first."

"Fine," Grandpa said. He put the little TV back into his bedroom.

"I'm sorry I fussed about the cookies," Benny's mom told his dad.

"I'll eat in the kitchen," Mr. Holt promised. "I did drop crumbs."

They kissed.

"I'll wipe my feet next time," Benny told his mother. "And dust the dirt off my jeans."

"Thank you," Mrs. Holt said. "I'm sorry I yelled at you."

She looked around the crowded garage. "We don't have room for all this stuff."

Dad nodded. "I can't even get to my workbench," he pointed out.

"We could have a yard sale," Benny suggested. "Like Mrs. Wong did, last summer. Sell the old furniture."

"I don't have time," his mother said. "I have to can my tomatoes while they're ripe."

"I have to work," Mr. Holt told them. "Lots of overtime at the plant right now."

They both looked at Grandpa.

"I'm still busy working on the election."

They all turned to Angie. She made a face. "I don't want to do it," she wailed. "Stand around all day in the hot sun?"

"I'll do it," Benny told them. "If I can keep some of the money."

"You're too little," Angie said.

Mrs. Holt shook her head. "If you can win a new living room set for me, you can run a yard sale," she decided. "And you can keep all the money. You deserve it!"

BELIEVE IT!

Benny spent all day Friday going through his closet. He collected his old trucks.

"Save one for Kevin," Mom suggested.

He gave the red truck to Kevin, but the rest went to the yard sale. He cleaned out old games and model planes.

Angie gave him a dollhouse and a whole stack of dolls. Grandpa found some slacks that didn't fit, and Mom had a stack of clothes, too. Dad added some shirts. "Must have shrunk," he explained. "I can't button them anymore."

"Ha," Benny's mother said. "I think it's too many peanut butter cookies." She patted Mr. Holt's stomach, and they both laughed.

Benny thought about selling his old bike, but decided he'd better keep it for Kevin. He could paint over the scratch. They'd buy a new tire. Kevin would like it.

Benny used some of Grandpa's paint and cardboard to make big signs. "Yard Sale Saturday: 110 Tulip Street."

He posted one at each end of the street, and one in front of the house.

On Saturday morning Benny got up very early. He was too busy for breakfast. His mother gave him a warm blueberry muffin to eat while he carried out clothes.

Murray rode by and stopped to watch.

"Now you're cleaning the house, too?" he shouted. "Baby-sitting wasn't enough?"

"I'm having a yard sale," Benny told him. "I'm going to earn money to buy a new bike."

"I'll believe it when I see it." Murray laughed as he rode away.

Benny set up the card table on the front lawn. He stacked all the clothes on the table and put the toys in front. It took him six trips to carry it all out.

Benny and Grandpa and Dad moved all the old furniture out onto the driveway. Then Dad went to work. Grandpa left to shake hands and ask people to vote.

Benny kept on working. He set the old lamps out so people could see them.

His mother brought out some of her ripe tomatoes. "You can sell these, too," she told him.

Cars began to pull up. People walked by and saw the sign and stopped, too.

Women looked through the clothes and

picked out what they wanted. Two kids fought over the trucks. A little girl fell in love with the dollhouse. A bald-headed man decided Grandpa's old slacks were just the right size.

The ripe red tomatoes sold quickly.

Benny collected the money and put it all into a shoe box.

A skinny man in jogging shorts bought the lamps.

A short lady in striped pants looked at the couch. "It has a hole in the cushion," she pointed out. "Sixty dollars is too much. I'll give you twenty-five."

"You can make a new cover for the cushion," Benny told her. "Forty-five."

"So I can," she agreed. "But that will take new material. Forty dollars."

"It's a deal," Benny said. They shook hands. Benny helped her put the couch into the back of her pickup truck.

A gray-haired lady bought the tables.

Two girls bought the rest of the dolls.

Nobody wanted the brown chair.

One little boy with curly hair stood a long time, staring at a model airplane.

"Want it?" Benny asked. "It's only fifty cents."

The little boy took his thumb out of his mouth and shook his head.

"No money, huh?" Benny said.

The little boy nodded.

Benny looked around. Almost everything had sold. Most of the people had gone.

"Here," he said. "Take it anyhow."

The little boy grinned. He picked up the toy plane and hurried down the street.

When everyone had left, Benny folded up the card table and put it away. He pulled the brown chair back into the garage. If he ever wanted to be alone, he knew where to sit.

"How much did you make, Benny?" Angie asked. She sounded a little bit sorry she

hadn't held the yard sale herself. "Is it enough?"

Benny took his money box into the living room, remembering to wipe his feet first.

His mother left her canning, and Angie looked over his shoulder. Benny sat down on the new couch and counted his money.

"One hundred and fifty-four dollars and thirty cents," he said proudly.

"I didn't think you'd make that much." Angie sounded surprised.

"The furniture did it," he told them. "Is this enough to get a new bike?"

"I think so," his mother said. "Let me put Kevin down for his nap. Then I'll take you down to the bike store at the mall. They have a big stock to choose from. Angie can watch the baby and my canning."

Angie shrugged. "Oh, all right. I guess you earned it."

By the time Kevin went to sleep, Grandpa had come home. "I think we're going to win the election," he said. "I'm good at shaking hands."

"Come to the bike store with us," Benny said.

Grandpa and Benny and Mom took the bus to a big shopping mall. They went into a store with lots and lots of new bikes.

Red ones and black ones.

Blue ones.

Big blue mountain bikes.

Benny walked up and down, admiring all the bikes. But he knew the one he wanted. The big blue mountain bike with strong tires.

He checked the tag and his stomach did a flip-flop. He didn't have enough money!

"What's wrong?" Mrs. Holt asked.

Benny couldn't answer. He pointed to the price tag, his lips quivering.

A salesman hurried up. "Can I help you?"

"Hmm," Grandpa said. "I think the discount store down the street has bikes on sale, Benny. We can check there."

"Wait," the salesman said. "We have bikes on sale, too."

He took them to the back of the store, where several bikes had red tags.

Benny saw a mountain bike—a blue, shiny mountain bike, and his heart lifted. "That's the one," he said.

It even had streamers on the handlebars, and a balloon tied to the back of the seat.

He checked the price tag. This was better!

"I'll take it," Benny said.

"Look over here," Mrs. Holt called. "You need one of these. I'll pay."

Benny looked at the rack of bike helmets. He picked out a sporty blue and black helmet, to match his new bike.

The salesman punched buttons on his cash register. Mrs. Holt took the sales papers and put them into her purse. Benny put on his helmet, just like a real pro, and pushed his new bike to the door.

"You take the bus," Grandpa told Mrs.

Holt. "I'll walk with Benny on the side streets, so he can ride his bike home."

"Watch out for traffic," she told them. Then she kissed Benny and admired the bike one more time. "Pretty," she said.

"Pretty? It's perfect!" Benny told her.

With Grandpa beside him, Benny walked his bike across the busy intersection, then turned into a side street. He jumped on his bike, wobbling only a little. This was one big bike! He could hardly reach the pedals.

Could this bike zoom ahead! Benny reached Tulip Street in no time. He rode his bike very fast down the length of the street. The streamers flapped in the wind, and the balloon floated behind him.

Melissa stared at the new bike. "Wow," she said. "Want to ride with me?"

"Later," Benny told her.

Murray rode by on his bike, the one with the scratch. He looked at Benny's new bike. He didn't say anything.

"Ha," Benny said. "Believe it!"

Mrs. Wong waved. Mrs. Morales's dog barked at him. Benny just laughed. "Can't catch me," he called.

Benny rode to the park and over the sand hills. His new bike climbed the hills easily. It flew down them like a big bird. Benny felt the wind on his face and heard the streamers fluttering. It made him want to shout.

"What a bike!" Benny yelled.

Cheryl Zach was born in Clarksville, Tennessee, and, as a child of a career army father, led a gypsy's youth, changing schools ten times in twelve years. After receiving her bachelor's and master's degrees in English from Austin Peay State University in Clarksville, Ms. Zach taught high school English for six years. Now a full-time writer, she has published nineteen books in hardcover and paperback original, both fiction and nonfiction. About *Benny and the Crazy Contest*, her first book for Bradbury, she writes, "I suspect what readers will remember about this book is Benny, who walked into my mind, full grown so to speak, and I fell in love with him. Benny is funny and determined and kindhearted and never gives up. In person, you'd like him."